KATE GREENAWAY'S MARIGOLD GARDEN

Pictures and Rhymes
By
KATE GREENAWAY

Grange BOOKS

Reprinted in 1993 by
Grange Books
An imprint of Grange Books PLC
The Grange
Grange Yard
London
SE1 3AG

ISBN 1 85627 540 X

Printed in Spain

Gráficas Reunidas, S. A.

MARIGOLD GARDEN

BY KATE GREENAWAY

YOU little girl,
You little boy,
With wondering eyes,
That kindly look,
In honour of
Two noble names
I send the offering
Of this book.

SUSAN BLUE

OH, Susan Blue,

How do you do?

Please may I go for a walk with you?

Where shall we go?

Oh, I know—

Down in the meadow where the cowslips grow!

BLUE SHOES

LITTLE Blue Shoes

Mustn't go

Very far alone, you know.

Else she'll fall down,

Or, lose her way ;

Fancy—what

Would mamma say?

Better put her little hand

Under sister's wise command.

When she's a little older grown

Blue Shoes may go quite alone.

TO THE SUN DOOR.

THEY saw it rise in the morning,
   They saw it set at night,
And they longed to go and see it.
   Ah! if they only might.

The little soft white clouds heard them,
   And stepped from out of the blue ;
And each laid a little child softly
   Upon its bosom of dew.

And they carried them higher and higher,
   And they nothing knew any more.
Until they were standing waiting,
   In front of the round gold door.

And they knocked, and called, and entreated,
   Whoever should be within ;
But all to no purpose, for no one
   Would hearken to let them in.

THE DAISES.

YOU very fine Miss Molly,
   What will the daises say,
If you carry home so many
Of their little friends to-day?

Perhaps you take a sister,
   Perhaps you take a brother,
Or two little daises who
   Where fond of one another.

GOING TO SEE GRANDMAMMA

LITTLE Molly and Damon
  Are walking so far,
For they're going to see
  Their Kind Grandmamma.

And they very well know,
  When they get there she'll take
From out of her cupboard
  Some very nice cake.

And into her garden
  They know they may run,
And pick some red currants,
  And have lots of fun.

So Damon to doggie
  Says, "How do you do?"
And asks his mamma
  If he may not go too.

THE DANCING FAMILY.

PRAY let me introduce you to
    This little dancing family ;
For morning, afternoon, and night,
    They danced away so happily.

The twirled round about,
    They turned their toes out ;
The people wondered what the noise
    Could all be about.

They danced from early morning,
    Till very late at night ;
Both in-doors and out-of-doors,
    With very great delight.

And every sort of dance they knew,
    From every country far away ;
And so it was no wonder that
    They should keep dancing all the day.

So dancing—dancing—dancing,
    In sunshine or in rain ;
And when they all left off,
    When then—they all began again.

WISHES

OH, if you were a little boy,
    And I was a little girl—
Why you would have some whiskers grow,
    And then my hair would curl.

Ah ! if I could have whiskers grow,
    I'd let you have my curls ;
But what's the use of wishing it—
    Boys never can be girls.

STREET SHOW.

PUFF, puff, puff. How the trumpets blow.

All you little boys and girls come and see
   the show.

One – two – three, the Cat runs up the
   three ;

But the little Bird he flies away —

"She hasn't got me!"

WHEN WE WENT OUT WITH GRANDMAMMA.

WHEN we went out with Grandmamma—
    Mamma said for a treat—
Oh, dear, how stiff we had to walk
    As we went down the street.

One on each side we had to go,
    And never a laugh or loll ;
I carried Prim, her Spaniard dog,
    And Tom—her parasol.

If *I* looked right—*if Tom* looked left—
  "Tom—Susan—I'm ashamed ;
And little Prim, I'm sure, is shocked,
  To hear such naughties named."

She said we had no manners,
  If we ever talked or sung ;
"You should have seen," said Grand-
    mamma,
  "*Me* walk, when *I* was young."

She told us—oh, so often—
  How little girls and boys,
In the good days when she was young,
  Never made any noise.

She said they never wished then
  To play—oh, no, indeed!
They learnt to sew and needlework,
  Or else to write and read.

She said her mother never let
  Her speak a word at meals ;
"But now," said Grandmamma, "you'd
    think
  That children's tongues had wheels.

"So fast they go—clack, clack, clack ;
  Now listen well, I pray,
And let me see you both improve
  From what I've said to-day."

TO MYSTERY LAND.

OH, dear, how will it end?
Peggy and Susie how naughty
   you are.
You little know where you are,
Going so far, and so high,
Nearly up to the sky.
Perhaps it's a Giant who
   lives there,
And perhaps it's a lovely
   Princess.
But you very well know
You've no business to go ;
You'll get yourselves into a mess.

Oh, dear, I'm sure it is true ;
Whatever on earth can it matter
   to you?
For you know it—oh, fie—
That it's naughty to pry
Into other's affairs—
Into other folks houses to go,
Where you know
You're not asked.
So you'd better come back
While there's time, it is plain.
Go home—and be never
So naughty again.

FIRST ARRIVALS.

IT is a Party, do you know,
And there they sit, all in a row,
Waiting till the others come,
To begin to have some fun.

Hark! the bell rings sharp and clear,
Other little friends appear ;
And no longer all alone
They begin to feel at home.

To them a little hard is Fate,
Yet better early than too late ;
Fancy getting there forlorn,
With the tea and cake all gone.

Wonder what they'll have for tea ;
Hope the jam is strawberry.
Wonder what the dance and game ;
Feel so very glad they came.

Very Happy may you be,
May you much enjoy your tea.

LITTLE PHILLIS.

I AM a very little girl,
  I think that I've turned two ;
And if you'd like to know my name
  I'd like to tell it you.

They always call me baby,
  But Phillis is my name.
No no one ever gave it me,
  I think it only came.

I've got a pretty tulip
  In my little flower-bed :
If you would like I'll give it you
  It's yellow, striped with red.

I've got a little kitten, but
  I can't give that away,
She likes to play with me so much ;
  She's gone to sleep to-day.

And I've got a nice new dolly,
  Shall I fetch her out to you?
She's got such pretty shoes on,
  And her bonnet's tirmmed with blue.

You'd like to take her home with you?
  Oh, no, she mustn't go :
Good-bye I want to run now,
  You walk along so slow.

FROM MARKET.

OH who'll give us Posies,

And Garlands of Roses,

To twine round our heads so gay?

For here we come singing,

And here we come bringing

You many good wishes to-day.

From market—from market—from market—

We all come up from market.

THE FOUR PRINCESSES.

FOUR Princesses lived in a Green Tower—
   A Bright Green Tower in the middle of the sea;
And no one could think—oh, no one could think—
   Who the Four Princesses could be.

One looked to the North, and one to the South,
   And one to the East, and one to the West;
They were all so pretty, so very pretty,
   You could not tell which was the prettiest.

Their curls were golden—their eyes were blue,
    And their voices were sweet as a silvery bell ;
And four white birds around them flew,
    But where they came from—*who* could tell?

Oh, who could tell? for no one knew,
    And not a word could you hear them say.
But the sound of their singing, like church bells ringing,
    Would sweetly float as they passed away.

For under the sun, and under the stars,
    They often sailed on the distant sea ;
Then in their Green Tower and Roses bower
    They lived again—a mystery.

IN AN APPLE TREE.

IN September, when the apples are red,
To Belinda I said,
'' Would you like to go away
To Heaven, or stay
Here in this orchard full of trees
All your life? '' And she said, '' If you please
I 'll stay here—where I know,
And the flowers grow.''

WHEN YOU AND I GROW UP.

WHEN you and I
Grow up—Polly—
   I mean that you and me,
Shall go sailing in a big ship
   Right over all the sea.
We'll wait till we are older,
   For if we went to-day,
You know that we might lose ourselves,
   And never find the way.

THE LITTLE LONDON GIRL.

IN my little Green House, quite content am I,

When the hot sun pours down from the sky ;

For oh, I love the country—the beautiful country.

Who'd live in a London street when there's the country?

I live in a London street, then I long and long

To be the whole day the sweet Flowers among.

Instead of tall chimney-pots up in the sky,

The joy of seeing Birds and Dragon Flies go by.

At home I lie in bed, and cannot go to sleep,
For the sound of car-wheels upon the hard street ;
But here my eyes close up to no sound of anything
Except it is to hear the nightingales sing.

And then I see the Chickens and the Geese go walking ;
I hear the Pigs and the Ducks all talking.
And the Red and the Spotted Cows they stare at me,
As if they wondered whoever I could be.

I see the little Lambs out with their mothers—
Such pretty little white young sisters and brothers.
Oh, I'll stay in the country, and make a daisy chain,
And never go back to London again.

TO BABY.

OH, what shall my blue eyes go see?
   Shall it be pretty Quack-Quack to-day?
Or the Peacock upon the Yew Tree?
   Or the dear little white Lambs at play?
      Say Baby.
For Baby is such a young Petsy,
   And Baby is such a sweet Dear.
And Baby is growing quite old now—
   She's just getting on for a year.

THE WEDDING BELLS.

THE Wedding Bells were ringing,
   And Monday was the day,
And all the little ladies
   Were there so fresh and gay.

And up—up—up the steps they went,
   The wedding so fine to see ,
And the Roses were all for the Bride,
   So pretty—so pretty was she.

WILLY AND HIS SISTER.

WILLY said to his sister
  "Please may I go with you?"
She said, "You must behave
  Very nicely if you do."

"Please will you take me then
  To look at the mill?"
"Yes," she said, "because you are
  So very good—I will."

"The miller he is
  So very white and kind ;
And sprinkled all over
  With the flour they grind.

"And the big heaps of corn
  That lie upon the floor ;
He will let me play with those,
  I am quite sure.

"I like to hear the wheel
  Make such a rushing sound,
And see the pretty water
  Go round, and round, and round.

"So take me to the mill,
  For then you shall see
What a very, very good boy
  I really mean to be."

HAPPY DAYS.

" ARE you going next week to see Phillis and Phoebe?
    Phillis on Monday will be just fourteen.
She says we shall all have our tea in the garden,
    And afterwards have some nice games on the green.

" I wanted a new frock, but mother said, 'No,'
    So I must be content with my old one you see.
But then white is so pretty, and kind Aunt Matilda
    Has sent down a beautiful necklace for me."

" Oh, yes, I am going, and Peggy is going,
    And mother is making us new frocks to wear ;
I shall have my red sash and my hat with pink ribbons—
    I know all the girls will be smart who are there.

" And then, too, we're going to each take a nosegay—
    The larger the better—for Phillis to say
That all her friends love her, and wish her so happy,
    And bring her sweet flowers upon her birthday.

" And won't it be lovely, in beautiful sunshine,
    The table spread under the great apple tree,
To see little Phillis—that dear little Phillis—
    Look smiling all round as she pours out the tea!"

THE LITTLE QUEEN'S COMING.

WITH Roses—red Roses,
  We'll pelt her with Roses,
And Lilies—white Lilies we'll drop at
    her feet ;
  The little Queen's coming,
  The people are running—
The people are running to greet and
    to meet.

Then clash out a welcome,
  Let all the bells sound, come,
To give her a welcoming proud and
    sweet.
  How her blue eyes will beam,
  And her golden curls gleam,
When the sound of our singing rings
    down the street.

AT SCHOOL

FIVE little Girls, sitting on a form,
Five little Girls, with lessons to learn ;
Five little Girls, who, I'm afraid,
Won't know them a bit when they have to be said.

For little eyes are given to look
Anywhere else than on their book ;
And little thoughts are given to stray
Anywhere—ever so far away.

ON THE WALL TOP.

So high—so high on the wall we run,
The nearer the sky—why, the nearer the sun.
If you give me one penny, I'll give you two,
For that's the way good neighbours do.

ON THE WALL TOP.

DANCING and prancing to town we go,
On the top of the wall of the town we go.
Shall we talk to the stars, or talk to the moon,
Or run along home to our dinner so soon?

THE UNGRATEFUL LAMB.

NOW, Lamb, no longer naughty be,
Be good, and homewards come with me.
Or else upon another day
You shall not with the daisies play.

Did we not bring you, for a treat,
In the greet grass to frisk your feet?
And when we must go home again
You pull your ribbon and complain.

So little Lamb be good once more,
And give your naughty tempers o'er.
Then you again shall dine and sup
On daisy white and buttercup.

MAMMAS AND BABIES.

"MY Polly is so very good,
   Belinda never cries ;
My Baby often goes to sleep,
   See how she shuts her her eyes.

"Dear Mrs. Lemon tell me when
   Belinda goes to school ;
And what time does she go to bed;"
   "Well, eight o'clock's the rule.

"But now and then, just for a treat,
   I let her wait awhile ;
You shake your head—why, wouldn't
      you:
   Do look at Baby's smile!

"Dear Mrs. Primrose will you come
    One day next week to tea?
Of course bring Rosalinda, and
    That darling—Rosalie."

"Dear Mrs. Cowslip, you *are* kind ;
    My little folks, I know,
Will be so very pleased to come ;
    Dears—tell Mrs. Cowslip so.

"Oh, do you know—perhaps you've not
        heard—
    She had a dreadful fright ;
My Daisy with the measles
    Kept me up every night.

"And then I've been so worried—
    Clarissa had a fit ;
And the doctor said he couldn't
    In the least account for it."

MY LITTLE GIRLIE.

LITTLE girlie tell to me
What your wistful blue eyes see?
Why you like to stand so high,
Looking at the far-off sky.

Does a tiny Fairy flit
In the pretty blue of it?
Or is it that you hope so soon
To see the rising yellow Moon?

Or is it—as I think I've heard—
You're looking for a little Bird
To come and sit upon a spray,
And sing the summer night away?

TIP-A-TOE.

TIP-A-TOE,

See them go ;

One, two, three—

Chloe, Prue, and me ;

Up and down,

To the town.

A Lord was there,

And the Lady fair.

And what did they sing?

Oh, "Ring-a-ding-ding;"

And the Black Crow flew off

With the Lady's Ring.

THE CATS HAVE COME TO TEA.

WHAT did she see—oh, what did she see,
As she stood leaning against the tree?
Why, all the Cats had come to tea.

What a fine turn out—from round about,
All the houses had let them out,
And here they were with scamper and shout.

"Mew—mew—mew!" was all they could say,
And, "We hope find you well to-day."

Oh, what should she do—oh, what should she do,
What a lot of milk they would get through ;
For here they were with "Mew—mew—mew!"

She didn't know—oh she didn't know,
If bread and butter they'd like or no ;
They might want little mice, oh! oh! oh!

Dear me—oh, dear me,
All the cats had come to tea.

UNDER ROSE ARCHES.

UNDER Rose Arches to Rose Town—
   Rose Town on the top of the hill ;
For the Summer wind blows and music goes,
   And the violins sound shrill.

Oh, Roses shall be for her carpet,
   And her curtains of Roses so fair ;
And a Rosy crown, while far adown
   Floats her long golden hair.

Twist and twine Roses and Lilies,
   And little leaves green,
   Fit for a queen ;
Twist and twine Roses and Lilies.

Twist and twine Roses and Lilies,
   And all the bells ring,
   And the people sing ;
Twist and twine Roses and Lilies.

THE TEA PARTY.

IN the plesant green Garden
   We sat down to tea ;
"Do you take sugar?" and
   "Do you take milk?"
She'd got a new gown on—
   A smart one of silk.
We all were as happy
   As happy could be,
On that bright Summer's day
   When she asked us to tea.

   When she asked us to tea.

A GENTEEL FAMILY.

SOME children are so naughty
    And some are very good ;
But the Genteel Family
    Did always what it should.

They put on gloves when they went out,
    And ran not in the street ;
And on wet days not one of them
    Had ever muddy feet.

They they were always so polite,
   And always thanked you so ;
And never threw their toys about,
   As naughty children do.

They always learnt their lessons
   When it was time they should ;
And liked to eat up all their crusts—
   They were so very good.

And then their frocks were never torn,
   Their tuckers always clean ;
And their hair so very tidy—
   Always quite fit to be seen.

Then they made calls with their mamma,
   And were so very neat ;
And learnt to bow becomingly
   When they met you in the street.

And really they were everything
   That children ought to be ;
And well may be examples now
   For little you—and me.

BABY MINE.

BABY MINE.

BABY mine, over the trees ;
   Baby mine, over the flowers ;
Baby mine, over the sunshine ;
   Baby mine, over the showers.

Baby mine, over the land ;
   Baby mine, over the water.
Oh, when had a mother before
   Such a sweet—such a sweet, little daughter!

FROM WONDER WORLD.

OUT of Wonder World I think you
    come ;
For in your eyes the wonder comes
    with you.
The stars are the windows of Heaven,
And sometimes I think you peep
    through,
Oh, little girl, tell us do the Flowers
Tell you secrets when they find you all
    alone?
Or the Birds and Butterflies whisper
Of things to us unknown?

Or do angel voices speak to you softly,
When *we* only hear a little wind sigh ;
And the peaceful dew of Heaven fall upon you,
When *we* only see a whitle cloud passing by?

MISS MOLLY AND THE LITTLE FISHES.

OH, sweet Miss Molly,
You're so fond
Of Fishes in a little Pond.
And perhaps they're glad
To see you stare
With such bright eyes
Upon them there.
And when your fingers and your thumbs
Drop slowly in the small white crumbs,
I hope they're happy. Only this—
When you've looked long enough, sweet miss,
Then most beneficent young giver,
Restore them to their native river.

LITTLE GIRLS AND LITTLE LAMBS.

In the May-time flowers grow ;
Little girls in meadows go ;
Little lambs frisk with delight,
and in the green grass sleep at night.
Little birds sing all the day,
Oh, in such a happy way!
All the day the sun is bright,
Little stars shine all the night.
The Cowslip says to the Primrose,
"How soft the little Spring wind blows!"
The Daisy and the Buttercup
Sing every time that they look up.
For beneath the sweet blue sky
They see a pretty Butterfly ;
The Butterfuly, when he looks down,
Says, "What a pretty Flower Town!"

THE LITTLE JUMPING GIRLS.

JUMP—jump—jump—
Jump away
From this town into
The next, to-day.

Jump—jump—jump—
Jump over the moon ;
Jump all the morning,
And all the noon.

Jump—jump—jump—
    Jump all night ;
Won't our mothers
    Be in a fright?

Jump—jump—jump—
    Over the sea ;
What wonderful wonders
    We shall see.

Jump—jump—jump—
    And leave behind
Everything evil
    That we may find.

Jump—jump—jump—
    Jump far away ;
And all come home
    Some other day.

ON THE BRIDGE.

If I could see a little fish—
That is what I just now wish ;
I want to see his great round eyes
Always open in surprise.

I wish a water-rat would glide
Slowly to the other side ;
Or a dancing spider sit
On the yellow flags a bit.

I think I'll get some stones to throw,
And watch the pretty circles show.
Or shall we sail a flower-boat,
And watch it slowly—slowly float?

That's nice because you never know
How far away it means to go ;
And when to-morrow comes, you see,
It may be in the great wide sea.

CHILD'S SONG.

THE King and the Queen were riding
    Upon a Summer's day,
And a Blackbird flew above them,
    To hear what they did say.

The King said he liked apples,
    The Queen said she liked pears.
And what shall we do to the Blackbird
    Who listens unawares.

BALL.

ONE—two, is one to you ;
One—two—three, is one to me.
Throw it fast or not at all,
And mind you do not let it fall.

RING-A-RING.

RING-A-RING of little boys,
Ring-a-ring of girls,
All around—all around,
Twists and twirls.

You are merry children ;
"Yes, we are."
Where do you come from?
"Not very far.

"We live in the mountain,
We live in the tree ;
And I live in the river-bed,
And you won't catch me!"

FAIRY Blue Eyes,
   And Fairy Brown,
And dear little Golden Curls,
   Look down.
I say "Good-bye"—
   "Good-bye" with no pain—
Till some happy day
   We meet again!